Briggsy
Goes to
Camp

Linda McKinley
Illustrated by Dwight Nacaytuna

To order additional copies of this book, contact:
Xlibris
844-714-8691
www.Xlibris.com
Orders@Xlibris.com

ISBN:	Softcover	979-8-3694-1206-0
	EBook	979-8-3694-1205-3

Library of Congress Control Number: 2023922373

Print information available on the last page

Rev. date: 11/28/2023

Dedication

For
My favorite campers
Who didn't forget to write

Briggsy and Mama Tuba were packing Briggsy's tuba case, for his first trip away from home. "Do I have to go to camp?" he asked Mama Tuba. "Camp is fun," she said. "You'll see. Now, don't forget to write," and gave him a big hug!

SCHOOL BUS

CAMP HARMONY

Briggsy was surprised when he arrived at Camp Harmony the next day, and saw Toodle-oo-Pete, his clarinet pal from school. He felt better now, seeing a friendly face. "Awesome to see you too, Briggs," said Pete.

The campers were taken to their cabins. Briggsy and Pete were happy to be together in the Ninja Cabin. Briggsy said; "hey Pete, we can be Camp Harmony's Ninja Warriors." Pete said, "yeah, cool! I'll be Michaelangelo. Cowabunga!" Briggsy laughed and said, "ok, and I'll be Donatello!"

Boomer, a drum, was the camp leader and drum major for the band. "Welcome to Camp Harmony," he told them. "Today we'll be canoeing on the lake." "Yay," everyone clapped, except Briggsy. He was afraid of the water. "Don't worry Briggs," said Pete. "If you fall in, flip over and float on your back. That way, your insides won't get wet," and laughed. So did everyone else, except Briggsy. "Don't worry, we'll be wearing our life vests," said Boomer, which made Briggsy feel much better.

Briggsy was pleasantly surprised to find that canoeing wasn't so bad after all. The good news was, he didn't fall in the lake. Lunch afterward was hot dogs, fruit, and cupcakes with sprinkles. Yum!, he thought. My very favorites!

That afternoon the instruments practiced camp songs. Music always made Briggsy feel so upbeat and happy! Everyone agreed that their little band sounded pretty good.

A hike in the woods was scheduled for the next morning. Each camper was given a compass , "in case you get lost," Boomer explained. Once they were in the woods, Briggsy was busy looking at his compass, and did not realize the others had gone off and left him.

It was even spookier in the woods now, since the sun was hidden behind the trees. Just then, Briggsy heard a sound that made him almost jump out of his hiking boots!

Sounds like someone yelling, HELP!, he thought. He followed the sound, and saw Toodle-oo-Pete down at the bottom of a hill, stuck in a clump of bushes. I hope that's not poison ivy, thought Briggsy.

"Hang on," Briggsy hollered, and took a deep breath for his loudest "Oom pah pah!" He was relieved to see his fellow campers come running. They tied their shirts together to make a rope, and lowered it down so Pete could grab hold and be pulled to safety. Everyone cheered when Pete said, "I'm ok guys, just a few scratches."

That night around the campfire, they all celebrated with music, scary ghost stories, and s'mores. A wise ole owl in a nearby tree went "Whoo," making everybody jump! Briggsy said, "great teamwork today guys." Pete agreed. "Yeah, you guys are the best!"

Tomorrow they would be going fishing, and the next day, arts and crafts, and playing happy camp songs with the band! Mama Tuba was right, thought Briggsy. Camp IS fun! In fact, he couldn't wait to write home and tell her all about it!

Printed in the United States
by Baker & Taylor Publisher Services